Published by Smart Brown Girl Publishing
BHK, LLC.

Copyright © 2016 Jouelzy
All Rights Reserved
ISBN 978-0-69-221904-1

Cover Art Illustration by Josh Galvez
Cover & Book Design by Jouelzy

For the lights that guided me, allowing me to define my own reality and live without boxes.

Mom, Dad, and the ring of close family & friends who will recognize their light throughout this book.

Table of Contents

Send It On

by Jouelzy

I've amassed this thing called potential, though I realized it was something greater than that. There's just no word for it. That thing, girl. That thing. I got it. But I wanted to fight it. Paulo Coelho wrote a novel about it. That boy in The Alchemist damn near traveling the seven seas just to realize his treasure was right at home underneath his willow tree.

Normalcy I was seeking. The 9-5-work week with Friday night drinks with the girls. Saving up for the week long vacays to the touristy spots like Cancun and Jamaica. I wanted that. To an extent. More so the married at 25, kids by 27. That's really what I wanted. The love, the warmth, the comfort from my 6-foot-something, dark brown, blue collar worker husband, who would run me warm bubble baths and listen to soul music with me, while cuddling and kissing and kissing and cuddling. Yeah, that's what I want(ed). And I felt it slipping away with that thing they call potential. That thing that separates me from the rest. Makes me hard to understand. Has me marching to the beat of my very offbeat drum.

So I doubled back, took a break from my potential and set out to find that love. If it could all be so simple. Lauryn and Cee-Lo and D'Angelo and Billie H. and Mary J. and Bilal and definitely, Erykah had all already written the soundtrack to that sad love affair; and it wasn't none of the happy shit. Silly me, with an open heart I played the fool, looking for something that needed to find me first.

This is my tale of love and want.
Twenty odd years in the making.

...if I run Lord only know how far I and I will fall behind
Gotta find a better place, find a better space
So that I, so my life may be the one reason why...

Send it right back to you
Send it on.

Dear Mommy

I'm walking down this path just for you, Mommy. You're the only reason that I keep going. Too many days I just want to bow out gracefully, take a step over the ledge and fall like an angel backwards. But I can't, Mommy. Just for you, I can't.

My success is your success and I cannot let my failure be your own. So Mommy, I am no longer fighting for me. It doesn't seem worth it. I would rather die than know that my life will be a lonely life. This success, that has yet to come, is not my own. Its just for you Mommy. I guess at the top we shall trade our success with the other.

You forfeited your career for your family and in turn I shall take the career, just so you can have the whole pie. Cause, Mommy, I don't think there's enough ingredients for two. So I'll take my half just so you can have a whole. Cause maybe, just maybe, the happiness that will radiate from your whole will make its way to me and warm my heart too.

I just want to be warm like a freshly baked sweet potato pie. Golden brown, honey dripped graham cracker pie crust, warmed with the sweet filling on the inside. Just enough crispness to hold it all together. Just enough softness to make it all right. Just the way Daddy made it.

Mom I'm doing it all for you. This is no longer my life to live. I just want to make you happy. Cause I've cried enough tears for the both of our lifetimes. And you've shed enough tears for a thousand years of solitude. I just want to make you smile.

To my Mommy who never smiles. I just want to make you happy. I just ask that God not take that away too.

I Don't Know

I feel like someone dug their hand into my chest and squeezing my heart, pulling it up thru my throat. I didn't know that I had this much resentment built up, that the grudge really existed.

But then again, this has been the year of 'I don't knows', and I don't know how many more 'I don't knows' are left in me. I'm beyond being out of my comfort zone and as soon as I think I might be coming to terms with the fact that comfort has been snatched from underneath me, that feeling dissipates. It's like I took a dare and went skinny dipping. Someone snatched my clothes up and I'm left cold and naked with a spotlight on me. And as soon as I think I've found enough coverage to keep me decent, I look and realize that it's nowhere near enough to cover the vital parts.

I'm on a rollercoaster and I want off, while some cruel, cruel person is holding my eyelids open, so I can't even close them to ease the anxiety of the next sudden drop or turn. It's not fair but it's life, although I'm frustrated and anxious, I'm not mad. I let that go and put 'I don't know' in its place.

I called Dad today, conjured up enough energy to get past the: "who's this?"
"Solana, Dad" "Who?" "Solana, hello?"
"Solana? oh, what do you want?"
Then midway through the conversation, "who's this

again?"

I love the man, but damn it takes a lot of energy to hold a 5-minute conversation. All so I can feel complete because I told Dad that I love him, though I'm pretty sure he misses that part of the conversation too.

I called him, to get some things with my health insurance straightened out, and of course he directs me to call Mother, even though she has nothing to do with my health insurance. I call her and, of course, it's back to: "Call your father."

Sigh

"Oh, and he has news for you."
"News? What news? Is he finally getting some? He got a new boo?"
"Ha! Come on its your father. but really he has some news for you. Just ask him"

Back to calling Dad, "yo Mom says you have news for me." I didn't comprehend the first three times he said it and then when I finally got it, my heart dropped.
"Your brother, Nigel, is coming to visit me on Tuesday."
"My brother...who?"
"MY SON Nigel is coming to see ME on Tuesday."

I don't know, I don't know, I don't know, I don't know if I

can even say 'I don't know' one more time.

"You mean that boy that left 15 years ago is reappearing to come see you on Tuesday?' "Yes, MY SON is coming to see ME...so you want to come home and see him?"

I don't know, I don't know, I don't know, I don't know if I can even say I don't know one more time. I don't know how to explain this feeling in my chest. I don't know why I'm overcome with anxiety. I don't know what I'm afraid of.

Damn, I'm tired of the 'I don't knows'.
I really just don't know.

It's been 15 years.

15 years since I was that little loud mouth 6 year old, crying by the hutch at 16 Booker Terrace, looking up at my heroic big brother. He was heroic simply because he was my big brother, and he promised me that he would keep in touch and come back to visit me. It's been 15 years and I don't know if I want to let all of that go.

I don't know if I want to see him.

I'm scared that I might cry. I'm scared that all I'll have to say to this strange 33-year-old man is "Why didn't you keep your promise?" I'm scared that I'm going to see him and turn into that little 6-year-old crying by the hutch, except this time we'll be at 107 William Penn Drive. I'm scared I'll get my hopes and he won't come through. I'm scared I'll be open and vulnerable. I'm scared I won't get the closure I've always wanted.

I don't know if I want to see him.
I don't know if I really want to let it go.
I don't know if I want him back as my brother.
I don't know if there's anything there.

I've clung to this little piece of love I still have down at the bottom of my heart that has allowed me to even still refer to him as my big brother. I've clung to this little piece of love and I'm scared that it might all disappear when I see him, when I realize that he's not the same big brother whose sacred memories I've hung onto, and I'm not the same crying 6 year old he left by the hutch, that day of his high school graduation.

I just don't know. But I know I'm scared. I'm scared that I will regret not seeing him or that he just won't show up.

Funny, one of my roommates told me when I first met him that he thinks I should write. Write about my life. He was convinced my life was interesting and I would have a great story to tell. So I took his advice and started to write. I got a whole 7 pages and then I stopped. But last night I opened up that 7-page word document, with the intent of continuing but all I did was read it over. I had just highlighted the major events in my life and of course one of them was about my big brother. Funny how now it might be coming to a close. Finally.

....

I was six years old. It was the beginning of June 1994. I was sitting by the hutch in the dining room, crying. I didn't want anyone to see me cry because even at an early age I didn't want to appear vulnerable. My older half brother Nigel had just graduated from high school. We had just come from the graduation, and his mother was at the door. She came to take him back to Florida with her - less than an hour after his graduation. Nigel arrived downstairs with all his stuff, while his mom and other family were sitting on the couch. He has another little sister, she was about 10 or 11 at the time - a rail thin, brown skinned girl. I wanted to talk to her, but I was too ashamed of my tears and what I deemed as overly emotional behavior to move past the hutch in the dining room. So I sat there.

Nigel walked over to say goodbye to me. I tried to quickly wipe my face and play it off like my allergies were acting up. I started fake sneezing and coughing. I'm sure as a six-year-old this was all very exaggerated and clear to my brother. He saw right through it, as he leaned down to my level, all 6'1" of his mocha brown frame that I was so jealous of. I always wanted to be brown skin like him but instead I had pale high yellow skin that later on lead to

12

me being teased as a white girl. My brother leans over to hug me and the rush of emotions surges through me. I cry and let it flow.

Maybe I knew that I would never see him again. Never hug him again. There would never be another summer where on the day before school started, I would wait at the top of the steps for my dad to bring Nigel in the house. He would run up the steps to tickle me and twirl me around. I would no longer have the bragging right of having an older brother. I couldn't use him to back me in my elementary arguments of 'I'm going to tell my brother' or 'my brother gave me...', with the twist of my neck to my other kindergarten cohorts. I was losing someone I admired, whose telephone conversations I would eavesdrop on, breathing heavy on the other line.

My big brother Nigel, leaned over and promised me that next summer he would come back to see me. Promised me that he would keep in touch and that he loved me. I cried. Because I knew that day that he had broken my heart. At six years old a boy had broken my heart.

I went to school the next day and at lunch I was overly frustrated with the stupid plastic pouches of chocolate milk they had given us with our peanut butter and jelly sandwiches. They always came with two slices of cheese, a combination I never understood, just chalked it up to being a white people thing. I don't like chocolate or milk

13

and never mastered the art of sticking your straw into that nasty plastic pouch. But that day I was insistent on it. I wanted to poke that pouch and break its seal like my heart had been broken. My way of proving a point at six years old. And I cried again.

I cried in front of the whole Ms. Cleary's kindergarten class. I cried because I knew Nigel would only send an anniversary card to my parents the next year. I would wait the whole summer and he wouldn't be there. He would disappear and then reappear on my 13th birthday with a phone call to the house. I would ask him what his favorite movie was (Friday), what his favorite sport was (basketball) and where he was (Iran). He would write me for the next 3 months then disappear again. He would reemerge, only through phone calls, when I was 17, married and a truck driver in Texas.

I cried because I knew he was no longer my big brother after that day. He was some man who had broken my heart, who 15 years later I no longer recognized his voice. I know nothing about him, other than he broke his promise and my heart. He set the hard path for the other men that attempt to enter into my life. And 15 years later I'm still trying to get past that crying six year old sitting by the hutch in the dining room. I cry.

Black Carrie(s)

I've never met a Black woman who idolizes herself in the vein of Carrie Bradshaw that I liked. Or better yet, that liked me.

I've come across about five of them in my short span of life thus far, and it's all pretty much been the same. They all really just don't like me, and it's never because I did anything personally to them. Must be something about my swagger. Do I move funny? Do I put them off ? I mean, not that I really care. It just strikes me as interesting that there's been this pattern.

"Sex and the City" was a cool enough show in my opinion, and I know plenty of women (and men) who loved the show. I get it, got it, moved on. I appreciate the witty value of each character, but there's just something wrong with a Black woman completely epitomizing Carrie Bradshaw. Granted, she had style. Patricia Field's style. It was cute. Single woman, over 30, doing her own thing in the rat race of New York City, I see the charm. But Carrie Bradshaw was quite indecisive and rather self-destructive in relationships. There were some great quotes made on that show. But it irked me to no end that she started everything off with a 'maybe'. At 30 do you not know anything concretely? Carrie Bradshaw can get away with that frivolous shit because she's a white woman. It's cute and chic, and she can ditzily skate through life on some "well, maybe you know good girls like the bad guys cause we like the thrill of the chase" while bobbing her newly coiffed blonde head from side to side.

'Maybe' denotes insecurity, which is probably another thing that endears Ms. Bradshaw to the women. I had a conversation with a homeboy, about the wackness of my previous male engagements. He said he felt that most mature people had outgrown or are in the process of outgrowing their insecurities. The maturation of shedding the layer of insecurities that often acts as a block to potential greatness or the ability to make sound decisions. But Carrie Bradshaw, she really was insecure. One of those people that would be highly offended if someone didn't like the outfit she had on. That's one very common trait of the Black women I've come across who like to walk in the vein of Ms. Bradshaw; do not not notice if they have on something new or dare to question their styling choices. You're a grown woman; at some point you should have learned to become comfortable enough with yourself, that you don't need accolades, like a 3 year old, every time you turn a corner. Everything you do, does not have to be noticed.

The (Black) Carrie Bradshaw complex, in my realm has all been encountered with women between the ages of 27-almost 30. They think that they are stylish but they're all single and faking happiness with it though they're really not. They've got careers and they aren't stupid women; they're all rather educated and I can more than give kudos where kudos is due. Obviously I haven't bothered to get

17

to know any of them too well, but I could surely assume that they all have some fantasy of a supposed relationship with a Big character, which is one big yawn. They could probably spend all day talking about how they're getting over their Big and he's so right, but so wrong for them, blah blah blah. And they're too busy self absorbing over their indecisiveness to notice the right man.

I know why they don't like me: because while they're too busy not making up their minds and trying to emulate a fictitious White woman who begins all her sentences with 'maybe', I say eff that and do what I want to do. Don't regret it, live it, learn it and move on.

Peach Cobbler

I had two packages in the mail today, one from each parent. My money is funny and they both decided to chip in a little to help.

There's a sanctity to handwritten letters. In a day and age when everyone has a smart phone, no one picks up their phone. I have friends who I've never even spoken on the phone to because everything is email and text messages. Handwritten letters are sacred.

Along with some financial substance. Both my parents sent me handwritten letters. Ah...I feel loved.

I call my Dad every once in a while. You know cause he doesn't think very often to call me, though I know he loves me. Since I can never be the one to just call and ask for money, there's the lead up conversation, and usually it's from me saying something off the wall and quirky.

So this time I call and ask my Father:

"What is it with men and their fascination in having a woman cook for them? I need some profound words of wisdom"

Of course, my Dad doesn't give me much of an answer and just responds with a chuckle and "so Solana how are you doing?" Lol, sometimes I wonder if he ever really listens to me.

"I'm fine Dad...but yo, I need some recipes...like how do you make peach cobbler? Cause I heard that the way to a guy's heart is through his stomach right? I need to up my cooking game son."

He just laughs and tells me the recipe for peach cobbler (which I'm finna to make this weetk) and tells me to use a pre-made pie crust.

"But I'm tryin to really, really, really impress this guy Dad, like I want him to be singing Stevie Wonder 'Overjoyed' after he has this cobbler...I need it to be official...so how do I make the pie crust myself?"

Yes I spent nearly an hour on the phone with my Father, getting the recipe for homemade peach cobbler with a homemade crust topping, before getting to the real point, though I think the peach cobbler became an even greater point than asking my Dad for an extra buck.

I got his package today. And it came with a letter.
A hand written letter:

Dear Sol,
Here's a little something to help ease your financial pain. As for food being a way to a man's heart that's a bunky non-sense! Because good cooks don't always make good lovers.
Being passionate about food says very little about the person,

it simply indicates he likes good food. Being honest and open
about what you stand for, what you will and will not accept in
a relationship or in a man is more endearing than a good meal.
The man must have values similar to yours.

If the way to man's heart is thru his stomach, he would marry
the waitress or cook at his favorite restaurant. So much for wise
words.

Love, Dad

I laughed so hard, I damn near cried. Okay, I shed a tear or two. I can be a bit sentimental.

It made me overwhelmingly happy. Not only cause that was hilariously funny coming from my Dad, who half the time I don't think is listening to me or he's dismissing me as his crazy and in-her-own-world-daughter. But because it shows that he does listen and care.

The little things are the best things. And that's going to be some good peach cobbler...(and no I'm not making it for no dude).

Zumunda

Hello good friends,

While I am dourly bored at work (they have me individually labeling 850 CDs, ah!), I decided to put my good ol' Blackberry pearl and thumbs to use, to entertain a few with what I feel would make a FABULOUS blog, except I can't really put myself on Broadway & 42nd like that. However recent happenings in my life must be discussed. The few who know me well, know that I have a great tendency to wear whatever I'm thinking on my face. So as to save me from some moron thinking he has the right to try his wack game on me because I'm sitting on the A train giggling to myself like a damn fool, I therefore am doing this email blog of sorts.

I've been told on several occasions, by those who were informed enough about my life, that my life is like one big episode of Sex and the City. I'm all 4 characters rolled up into one. No, not just Carrie. The random situations that I often find myself in cannot be denied. I'm even so tempted as to start a blog so I can detail my various tales. But I digress.

About 2 weeks ago, I brought in the deuce-deuce with a debaucherous bang! I was feeling myself, as one should on their day of birth. I find my day of birth to be a particularly grand one, so you know I was OD-ing in the moment. Apparently, I gave one young gentleman an offbeat lapdance. The lapdance I remember, the being offbeat part I don't know if I believe, being as the good friend who noted it should have saved me from myself, but again I digress. In the process of getting my Vita (see NERD "Lapdance" video) on, I knocked over an entire table of mixed drinks and such. But, 'come on baby it's my birthday' and I looked cute. Anyway this strapping young gentleman, who goes by the 'teh ghey' name of Frenchie, took my number and texts me a few days later with the usual disenchanting womp womp about my lips. I, of course, put him in his proper place. Quick shutdown, thanks.

Fast forward to a week later at 6 am and I get a text saying he woke up thinking about me and he feels crazy. Now I'm assuming the normal person would back away slowly and then run fast as hell away from one who texts them about what could be assumed as a potential wet dream after only encountering them for three hours, a week ago. But Soli B.? Nary one to turn down the potential for a great tale, used that moment to get a date out of him. I did remember that he was attractive, or I was at least hoping that the alcohol had not gotten to my better judgment. And my EBT card was low, the don't refill my food stamps till the 4th of the month. A free meal is a free meal, holla!

So the date goes down two days later. Monday night, he meets me in front of the Universal Records office. I was pleasantly surprised that he was good looking (so there, I know my last name, can walk straight and pick out a cute guy when I'm drunk!) And he was tall, 6'5 to be exact. I had forgotten that I had six inch heels on that night. Super bonus points. Carrying on, we hopped in a cab heading to dinner. After he asked what I do and I give him the run down, I returned the question. He laughed and said he'll tell me a little later. My immediate reaction was "I don't get down with that illegal shit." He just laughed.

"So what is it that you do?" I need to know, since he held out a bit earlier, I'm bracing for some wack hood mentality or even worse he's one of those Africans Chris Hansen's been chasing on Dateline. No bueno, homie. I wasn't prepared for what he had to say though.

"Well, 3 times a week, I take women out and entertain them for the night"
"What?!"
"Wealthy women that come into town and need company for the night, I take them out on dates."

The look on my face could not have been captured in a Kodak moment. I damn near shouted across the table, "So you're an escort? You get paid to 'entertain' women…"
"Nah sex isn't involved. I don't get down like that."
"You're a Black man with wealthy women throwing the cooch and money at you, and you always turn that down?"
"Some guys go for it, but that's not me. We hang out for the night. I don't go up to their hotel room with them."
"You don't have to be in a hotel room to bang pelvic bones."

26

He gives me the whole rundown about how these women are lonely, caught up with having the status of a wealthy husband and are resigned to living with the care and compassion…womp womp…so they take their husband's money to entertain themselves.

I can't believe it. This dude really makes his money as an escort! And of course, me of all people, picks him up. I really have no words for this revelation.

"So, you got a girlfriend?"
"Nah, but I was married."
"Huh?! Are you divorced."
"No, but we've been separated for 9 months."

"Damn I really pick them well. An escort who's married."

"Nah that part of my life is over, she took the house and I moved out."

Not only is he an escort, but he done jumped the broom. I am thoroughly entertained and can't stop laughing. My exceptional taste in men has led me to 'fetish4breasts', 'smack that ass', now it's 'Deuce Bigalow, Prince of Zumunda' himself. He knows I'm finding this absolutely hilarious and I know he's enjoying entertaining me. His Congolese behind is very charming, obviously as he has to be able to entertain these 'women friends' of his. I ask him how he ended up in America. He says he played professional basketball in France, and then a scout brought him out to Santa Monica to play basketball at a college, but he ended up having to leave.

"Umm…why did you have to leave?"
He laughed, "You're going to think I'm crazy"
Too late for that.
"I OD'd"

Is it just me, or is it really peculiar for a rather fresh off the boat African to use the term 'OD'. Something about him using that particular phrase struck me as odd. Maybe because he didn't sound at all African or Congolese, a rather quick assimilation to hood vernacular.

He was playing ball at this college in Santa Monica. Of course, all the hoes is throwing the pussy at him, etc.,. But he doesn't really move like that, so he wasn't taking the ladies up on their offers. He found himself in wild situations, with girls trying to get it in, but he always turned it down. There's this one girl who's trying to get it in and she happens to be the ex-girlfriend of some other "brolic" dude on campus. Frenchie and this chick are in the car just talking. Apparently he finds himself in these wild situations because he has a keen, sympathetic ear for his female counterparts. This girl is telling him about her life, they are having a deep conversation in a car, at night in front of brolic dude's dorm. Right.

"You know how the windows fog up at night if you sitting in the car?" Um no, I don't.

Folks thought they was getting it in cause the car windows was all fogged up and the brolic dude came down and tried to get rowdy. Since everyone in LA has gang affiliations, Frenchie didn't fight him. As he said, he didn't have energy to waste on "wack fools". His roommate, however, had "mad, mad love" (why did I feel like I was talking to a dude from Brooklyn?) and got down with the Bloods, decided to have his back and make something of it. Frenchie then transfers to a college in Upstate New York to avoid it becoming a big ordeal. He wasn't "fucking with the atmosphere" and so he bounced. "I hopped on a boat, came to New York City; I found Queens and fell in love with the city. And then I set out in a search to find my perfect lady who loved me without knowing I was a prince", he said with a perfect Congolese accent. Frenchie is funny. Then he started singing I am your Prince of Zumunda. Foolishness.

I had a good time. And the worst part, I genuinely like him. I think it's because Frenchie makes me feel like the real middle America, mall shopping, hanging out at Cheesecake Factory on Friday nights with my homegirls, suburban chick that I am. He beats me at being random and I love it! Plus for being a francophone he has the hood colloquialisms down pat. As he puts it, it's easy to learn the English of the hood because they only use the same words.

Oh boy, this will be an interesting one.

Umbrella
[eh-eh-eh]

There's a boy, I quite fancy. But he scares me simply because he's an Aquarius and he does those very Aquarian things, like keeping me at arms length. This arms length business is quite confusing and though it provides for great humor, it's murder to my insecurities.

The first tale of the absurdities was on the second date, when we went for the Guinness Book of World Records of longest dates by spending 14 hours with each other, though it didn't seem like that long. At the end of the date, in which to his credit he shows great chivalry by driving me back to Brooklyn from New Jersey, he ends the date by giving me what I like to term the "homie handshake!" Yes my friends, the "homie handshake". Not a full, gripping handshake even, but the three fingers curled back with the index finger pointing forward "dap" that's often exchanged amongst street acquaintances. Not even the dap that's given with a hug to suggest brotherly love, I simply got the three fingers. In turn, I looked at it with disgust. "What is this?", I belted out with a laugh. He then switched it into a full hood handshake, I laughed and resolved that the point was lost. Besides, I'm extra awkward when it comes to physical interaction, so I typically refuse to take the initiative. I'll just let it rock for now. Maybe he's just trying to be nice and respectful. But damn, can a sister get a hug?

The next date ended with me getting a hug. Finally a hug! But wait, wait, wait, why does this feel so sisterly? The mad tight, up top hug. He's hugging my shoulder blades. It feels quite....familial. I should be grateful though and appreciate the "respect." He's not trying to climb into my draws or bend me over on my porch. But a little hand slide or rub down the back never hurt nobody. Touché, till the next time my dear. Or at least I thought.

...

We're at his house and headed to the movie theatre, about 5 blocks away and there's a slight drizzle outside. Apparently he has a fear of rain, much like the wicked witch of the West, Evilene, from the Wiz. Where are the Black naked people dancing and jumping about, every time he walks out the door? I have yet to see them. Fear of messing up his shoes (will they melt?) has led me to having plenty of shit talking material. So thanks be to that.

It's not even legitimate rain, more like morning dew, a slight precipitation at the most. And what does he do? He immediately goes back into the house to get an umbrella. But oh no, not only does he come out with one oversized Mary Poppin-esque umbrella, that can fit an entire family but he also brings along a smaller one just for me. Am I bugging? Is this really happening? Should I feel flattered rather than the offense that's boiling up inside me right now? All I can do is laugh, cause this is sheerly hilarious. Let us break this down. TWO umbrellas. He keeps the larger one, which is enough for two to share when it's barely precipitating (because I refuse to call it rain). Really, if he was going to do all of that he could have given me the bigger one. Not that I would have taken it in the first place. Has he not heard of Rihanna? What kind of friend is he that I can't even stand under his umbrella-ella-ella-eh-eh-eh? I am sheerly confounded and amused. I refuse his attempts at handing me the smaller umbrella, as I enjoy the light drizzle and since Dorothy is my side chick, I just ease on down the road. You can be the scarecrow, without a brain (or a heart for that matter) and walk around with two umbrellas. Thank you and good night, my friend.

Friday Night
Lights

You know what's crazy?

Friday night, I'm sitting in the club with people who are enabling my future to be blindingly bright. Drinks are poured, music is right and I'm seated tapping my thumbs away while feeling some way.

I want to type out this emotion that's been lingering somewhere in the background.

Damn, I wish I could explain it. And somewhere the words escape me while the emotion settles no matter how far back I intend to push it. And it wasn't even love. Yet months later I'm left with a lingering resentment and beguilement that has rendered me unable to completely move on. Maybe because there was no real closure -- whatever that is.

I keep trying to convince myself that this wack negro only has a place - located somewhere between my sternum and left lobe - because I know I'm winning and he just made the most nonsensical choice of his life. How can one really disrespect me like that? And the more I think about it, the more it's like trying to fit the square in the triangle. It just ain't right and the "ain't right" is left knotted up right above my main artery knocking on my left lung.
Damn you for being so stupid. And if I didn't have any integrity or really believe that I am amazing, I might be so inclined to let you know about yourself. Though

that moment of ignorance seems so enticing, it's like the gleaming chitlins my grandma use to make with the reeking odor steaming forth from it.

I'm pushing this feeling back again. Awaiting for something far greater, that I really deserve, to absorb the ignorance that you penetrated into my heart. It's still sore, but healing.

October 11th

October 11, 2008

I am entirely frustrated. I don't know or even really understand how and at what point did my happiness get so wrapped up in your actions. It's running me up a wall that the simple inaction on your part can entirely sway my mood. I don't like it one bit. All the fun has been drained from the situation and I'm left felling like shit, because you can't even think to ask me how I'm doing. And I just keep hanging on because I feel like I need to get over myself and realize that I'm worth more. I need to learn how to not take it so hard. And maybe, just maybe, if I stick it out with you - I can cry out all my insecurities while you subconsciously play me. So then for the next man I'll be a better woman and know how to demand the respect I deserve from the door. Maybe I can figure out why I always get shorthanded in these situations and what I'm doing wrong. Cause I'm tired of feeling like I'm sinking and no one cares.

Press Delete

I sent this in the morning via BlackBerry Messenger:

I've decided that you and I can no longer have dealings with each other. Seriously. This situation isn't going to benefit me in any way. I stand to gain nothing. Other than experiencing what it's like to be the side chick, jumpoff whatever. And that's an experience I can do without.

And I don't want to be your faux friend either. Cause that's the same scenario as a jumpoff. So I'm deading it. Officially. And don't worry I'm not sad or melancholy about it.
It's all good in the hood.

I just rather spend time doing things that actually benefit me rather than sell myself short. So maybe next lifetime or some time after that we can just be cool. But for now I'd rather act like its Dec. 30th and I never met you.

He replies, of course, albeit 4 hours after he read it . Ah, the glory of messenger::
I agree with you to a T, I just don't want us to be enemies because of the way things played out.

Never one to not put the nail in the coffin, I say::
That is noble and all. But no need to worry about us being enemies, since there is no real reason for us to interact. Just press delete.

He complies. Deleted.

Perpendicular
Contradictions

I want to shake this feeling out of me. Scrub out the scent, readjust my self. I have this feeling right between my legs and just below the clasp of the button on my jeans that keeps reminding me of my drunkenness. The point of no return. I incurred another notch on the belt, I've desperately been trying to shorten. Damn, why can't I go back. I just don't want to feel like the victim. I was in my own home. That just don't feel right. It's easier just to be mad at myself then to point the finger at someone else. Open up a whole can of worms that I don't want to deal with. The finger pointing, back against the fence, throwing me under the bus, "you know you wanted it" commentary that leaves you cringing because you don't exactly remember everything that happened that night.

I should have been in more control. I should have stopped it sooner. I should have put the damn cup down. I should know myself. And this is what I've been dealing with since that last boy. You know the one I actually wanted to sleep with. I should know myself. But everything just keeps coming back glaring at me, like 'bitch, what the fuck is you doing?' I don't know anymore. And what I'm finding out just hurts my soul.

This is not a story I can go championing amongst my homegirls. I can't read him his rights because arguing with the ignorant just makes you lose your intelligence. There's nothing to be said. I keep trying to recount it to see why it happened. At what point did I write this into existence. Offer my hand out in a come hither motion. All I remember is shadows. Shadows in my bedroom, right after I had crashed in my bed from dispensing everything I had consumed that day into the toilet bowl. Another time where my mind and my body aren't moving in parallel motions. Perpendicular contradictions. I don't remember time frames. One minute I'm here; next minute it's black and a whole hour could have passed. Then I'm up and he's there. Why are you in my room, in my bed... on top of me? Why can't I just say no? Where is my voice? Didn't I just throw up? Is he really putting his mouth to mine? I had so many thoughts running through my head and not one of them came out. Other than, 'I'm too drunk for this shit' as I pantomimed in my dark room to find my underwear. My legs finally came to back to life and I was able to move my body off the bed. I had turned the light on but then quickly turned it off because I didn't want to realize what was really happening. The smirk on his face didn't help either. Let it sit in the darkness. Let it be a figment of my imagination. My salacious imagination. Turn the light off and exit stage right.

But no. He thinks it's all, all right. That was just the appetizer and there is a full meal awaiting. Son, I'm too drunk for this shit. I dived back into my bed and pull the sheets over me. Fuck, they smell like him. Why is he picking me up and pulling me out of my bed? Dear lawd. Lets walk to the door and end this. I'm too drunk for this.

I want to slap my head a million times. Replace his little comments with me saying no. But I didn't. I want to wash this feeling between my legs out of me because I keep waking up with the memory. He proved that I'm a dirty little whore. I have no limits, no boundaries. Dirty little me, I just want to scrub out of me. Took out the emotion, the sincerity, the intimacy. Yanked it from right under me.

It's easier just to be mad at myself rather than play the victim. Something about being the victim in my own home, with someone I know, just doesn't sit right. Then I keep having to replay if it was something I did or said. So I'll just be mad at me right now. Till I wash this dirty little feeling out of me. And then we can play, 'forget that memory.' It's not one that's needed.

(THE TALK)

Emphatic exhale. We talked. Exactly what I didn't want to do. But blinded with anger at myself and no easy way out, I concede when he shows up at my door. Twice. In the world of misogyny he seeks out my homeboy, the connector between the two of us, Sheldon, to discuss how he wants to "get at me." In the world of his ignorant bliss, my tight and drunk pussy seems quite indulgent and he wants to pursue. Never mind the fiancée that lives with him and whose medical school tuition bill he's fully funding. Or the more-than-a-jumpoff whom he's housing in New Jersey. Or the stripper in Long Island, who I've seen him 4 finger fuck with a titty in his mouth at the strip club. All women that I've met on his own accord. He wants to "get at me." Somehow I fit in line with this stable. The new conquest. So he rings Sheldon up the Monday after our dirty little drunken exchange. Sheldon tells him he needs to have a conversation with me, as a man, because his actions aren't acceptable and I'm not that type of chick. At 29 years, he can't seem to assess this for himself. So he promptly drives over to my house with Sheldon.

"No, I'm not answering the door.
He can't come into my house.
Come back in thirty minutes."

He comes back and we head to Peaches to eat and talk. He acts as if everything is hunky dory as I try to signal for Sheldon to not leave us. I don't want to have this conversation by myself. He keeps asking me how I'm doing. Tries to make innuendos about our future. As if there is a future.
"Do I drive?"
"Yes."
"Good to know, so I can let you drive my car sometime."

I guess that was suppose to get my panties wet, have me panting all over him and his Navigator, like 'Oh daddy, I get to drive your Navi.' Gun me.
"No, I don't like big cars."
"Oh."

We order. And then begin the bullshit conversation that left me not touching a drop of my food and him arrogantly picking at his chicken wings while he comes up with flip flop excuses and lies. I call his bluff.

"It's better if we no longer associate with each other."

He looks shocked. The man with the money never takes the L. Today you will.

"I feel violated. Couldn't you tell I was drunk. Why did you come into my bedroom? I just threw up. Bullshit, you had to taste that on my breath. Disgusting. You fuck mad bitches and then just want to stick your shit in me. Oh yeah, you thought about it, huh. I'm embarrassed. You couldn't approach me like a man. Don't accuse me of being attracted to you as if that is an excuse." I spewed all this at him as my face contorted into stank, disgust, and hatred all at once.

He then switches to low blows with a giggle and smirk on his face as he tells me that I need better middle men.
"Middle men? There's only one person we both talk to, stop talking in riddles. Sheldon?"
"Yeah, Sheldon, he told me that you're down for whatever." Bullshit. Lies.

We're in a public place. I can't yell. I can't jump across

the table and choke the life out of him. I can't gouge my fingernails into his cocked right eye that never seems to be in sync with his left. We're in public and the waitress is asking me if everything is okay. I curtly tell her yes. "Middle man? Sheldon? Testing my personal friendships? Fuck you and your bullshit. Fuck you and your lack of respect. You are a grown ass man that can't own up to your actions. You violated me and while I'm adult enough to accept my role in this. You were wrong. And you have to respect my feelings."

He plays around with his macaroni and cheese. Takes a scoop of collard greens. Chews loudly, then retorts that there's no point in discussing anything because I'm not compromising and I think everything he says is bullshit. He's sorry that I feel violated. He has a smug look of glee. The gotcha' bitch look. He could care less. Offering half apologies and low blows. I can't even look at him. I'm boiling as I realize I'm talking to a sociopath. He has no remorse as I walk out of the restaurant.

He has no remorse until he again talks to Sheldon who flat out tells him he's wrong. No remorse until he realizes he might lose face amongst his homeboys. Then he thinks to call me and offer an apology. An apology that I will not hear as I double tap the ignore button.

Send It On

It was written...

I like him. I like him a lot. So much so that I threw in the towel at 12 days cause I wanted to be close to him. I wanted to feel him. You have to say that sensually, "feeeeel." Drag out the 'e' and let your tongue glide over the 'l'. Yeah, *feeeeel*.

It was instantaneous. I fell and fell hard when he grabbed my hand and rubbed his palm into mine while he was telling me how much he likes Stevie. The wonders of my heart are in music and in that moment it fell right into his palm. Something electric. And I don't even like being touched. But somehow he did it just right. Caressed my palm with his tough skin, saying all the right things, without saying much.

I was overwhelmed. Cause he liked me too. We linked into each other's arms easy breezy and it just felt right. He's responsive and attentive. He emotes the same passion and thought with just as much intensity. Two weeks and the thought of him is pounding at my sternum while traveling up to my throat and leaving me smiling idly while walking down the street. Sprung. But he hesitates in trusting his emotions. He has thrown up his guard and is playing passive aggressive with my heart. Cause he scurred. And my intuition can see the set up from a mile away. I pray, please don't self destruct. Just take the leap of faith with me and I promise you will be well rewarded.

He's putting in more effort to concoct a reason why we can't be. Rather than just fall backwards with me. And I'm whispering to him like Norah Jones, *"baby please take off your cool cause I wanna see you, I wanna see you. Baby please don't be so cool I want to get to know you."* He knows that the only way he can adjudicate is to avoid. Because the moment he sees me he can't deny the emotions and just my presence melts his cool. Baby, just believe in me. I got your back. I got you.

2 weeks of hollow.

I'm infatuated. Lusting, loving, trying not to fall too far into - love - with a man who's doing all the wrong things, yet his presence makes it all feel so right. I've thrown in the towel on doing the right thing and decided to let my emotions reign supreme. We'll see how long it takes for me to click Lauryn Hill then scroll down to "Ex-Factor" in iTunes, or more appropriately, "When It Hurts So Bad."

Sigh. Exhale. Maybe I can create my own orchestra and sing this relationship into the existence of "He Loves Me (Lyzel in E Flat)" while he invites, ignites, co-writes, excites all those good and warm feelings into chorus. Can I live? I think my heart strings are creating a new soundtrack and I just want it to end in the right tune. Become a classic requiem of love and passion. Did I tell you how good this feels, when I know it's so wrong. Dangerous. I'm leading with my heart, my chest forever raised towards the sky.

Three Days Later

I want my heart back. I want back my emotions, my frustration, my mind, like, lust and passion. I want it all back because I'm left with emptiness the moment I gave it out to him. I'm trying to comprehend why I have such strong feelings that are so dually ignored. Can you like someone so much that you just avoid them? And then I'm left to play this silly game of moving on but not really. The come hither because you've realized you fucked up and lost a good thing. But I can't do that. I hate it. Abhor it. I want him. I want love, care and respect - from him. I want this feeling of melancholy to be over washed by a simple text of 'hello'. Something, anything. Care. Hold me. Wrap me up and make this uneasiness go away. I'm so over it. I know I deserve more with all the cliché conundrums of excelled womanhood I know apply to me. All I want to do is go crawling over to him. Shake him. Make him wake up and realize that I am it. Maybe I can drill all of this out of me with a tattoo म"झ यार करो.

The Weekend

Morning calls with my homegirl, Temi, and I trying to shake ourselves out of the abyss of caring, almost loving but really just liking (a rare occurrence for both of us) without any reciprocity. I've been playing this Anthony Hamilton song, "The Point of it All" trying to convince myself that the point of it all is exactly what I deserve and nothing less. So obviously, I need to stop settling for less. Something I already know, but for whatever reason I need the music to remind me. I was settling for a "Little Bit" and even though I love that song, being ignored is never the route for one who has so much to offer. It's a sad story that my heart is still telling me will have a happy ending but my mind is having a hard time reconciling with not taking the lapse in time personal and knowing better. That's what I really need. For my heart and mind to be in agreement with one another. And to be patient, the lacking virtue that's making it so hard for me to maintain right now. But for now I feel okay. Just alright. I think I may be finding the balance right around the corner. There are worse things to deal with and I just really need to refocus and not lose touch with reality. Maybe I should write down all the songs that explain the mixture of emotions I'm feeling right. All the soul singers who've caught my heart in between their cadences. Maxwell, would obviously be leading the pack and this whole deliberation could be wrapped up in "Playing Possum." If only I could make desperation sound so sexy maybe I could seduce him into growing and opening up.

Sunday

Hmmm, melancholy withdrawal still has me wavering in moments of impatience. I'm plotting for a melodramatic end if I don't get the smallest return of my emotional investment with him. I can write a treatment to the end as I see it in my head.

Wednesday. Late night. Sugarcane. Car parked to the east on the side that says 'NO Standing'. Government tags on his Chevy... End of the bar, he stirs with a Hennessey and Red Bull, blindly watching whatever is playing on the flat screen while soca blast in the background. Maybe I could be like the Lady in Orange, as I saunter over to his usual spot at the end of the bar. Orange buttterflies and aqua sequins encossed 'tween slight bossoms. I'm set for the kill . One last kiss. A few words.

And I leave. He dangles, hopelessly.
"You've lost something that you'll never find in another. I wish you all the happiness your mind & heart are open to. Read between the lines, my dear...I'm telling you - you've lost. A damn good thing."
Toodles, in my Purple Label heels.

This is the idea of an ending that really I never want to end. I'm still hopeless, like a penny with a hole in it, that I'll win with a little bit of patience and perseverance. Something grande is waiting for me on the other side. Maybe just on the other side of Labor Day.

The Morning After
I did as I said. I kept my word. Wednesday night. Got pretty. Lipgloss check. Hair bouncy. Kept it chic yet simple, even went and bought a new shirt. Had to make sure that tat was sunkissed and in good view. Then off I went to sucker punch the dude that left me high and dry

with a well of emotions as he sipped his drink at the end of the bar at Sugarcane. And, yes, the Purple Label pumps were on. Anxiety had settled into my stomach so I walked the distance from Atlantic Center because I needed to calm myself and fully own the moment, however it was to end. Of course, he was there. In the same seat per usual, fully uniformed - just as I had met him. Hmmm, did this whole engagement come full circle? Clearly my walk didn't fully calm my nervous, as I plopped down into the seat next to him and he asked "I can't get any love?" and I gave a curt "I guess." Hugs and it sucked that it felt so good, the warmth. *Exhale.*

I attempted to say goodbye, although I didn't sound as sultry and sexy as I envisioned in my head. I sounded more like a melancholy yet still giddy, 7th grader.

"I just wanted to say bye."

He didn't believe it, "like...really?" "Yes, really."

"People don't say goodbye. They usually say, see you later"

"No that's what we're doing now. So I'm cutting it off at the root" "Can we talk about it?"

Outside we go where we spend 90 minutes of deliberate pauses for him to think, me restating my sincerity for the 60 millionth time, and him stopping and pausing and stopping and pausing - for me to cling on to his slithers of "opening up to me." All while he pulls me in. Wrapped in warmth, I try to play cool with my arms crossed and averted looks, while he slides down my backside. We stop. Pause. Talk. Look. Kiss. Wince. Feel. Rise. Smooth. Anxious. Ending with a statement for him to open up and give it a try. He didn't trust that I was sincere. He notices the tattoo. It's Hindi for "love me" - suddenly it makes sense. Just believe. Dinner to be the next night.

I was holding my breath the whole conversation. I was hoping to get what I wanted but ready for the end I had set out for. Then I got what I wanted. At least for that moment. I just felt silly. Like really? Can I be happy? I want to question him to affirm my insecurities. Give me the guarantee, that would ruin the moment and turn into obligations. Damn, I like him. But I don't want to get my hopes back up in order to come crashing back down to the end of the bar at Sugarcane.

Thursday
We did dinner. Midnight. Traffic on the Manhattan bridge, coupled with his late work schedule landed as at a random restaurant in East Village, shortly after Cinderella's carriage turned back into a pumpkin. He looked miserable and delighted. A sniffling, tired mess that sorely needed to see a pillow and a soft bed. I felt a little bad, but he insisted he was okay and I just smiled, along for the ride. I just enjoy his presence. There's nothing special that we do. I just enjoy the feeling. The empty conversation. I ask. He replies. He feels. I move closer. He opened the car door for me. The little things make my heart flutter and my smile widen. I thanked him for dinner. He sniffled

with congestion. An offer of Vitamin C led him into my bedroom and comfortable on my bed. I play nurse for 10 minutes, amounting to me finding random object in my cluttered bedroom, before being pulled on top of him. Best yet. Not grand. But progress. And he talked to me while looking me in the eye.

Chills down my side as I ride, something that usually sends insecurities darting through my brain, but with him I just rode with it. And it felt so good. I want to make him chicken noodle soup and rub his back. Make him feel better. I'm so sprung, its sickening. He leaves at 6 am, right after pulling me in and kissing me on the neck. Shivers. Sigh. I like. Kiss goodbye to the tune of call you later and an arm full of tissues and Vitamin C. Can I be happy yet? I'm still scared.

Sunday

Deep deep deep sigh. I'm waking up with my heart on the verge of being stuck in my throat, thumping loudly at my sternum. I'm scared to believe now. After all that, I'm scared to get my hopes up. I'm so scared of the let down. Back to square one of waiting and pacing for that little slice of correspondence that says I'm thought of. I keep playing Adele's "Best for Last" because its exactly how I feel. I want him to say all of the right things, without a clue. Just like he did when we first met and fell into the others arms so easily. I just want to make it simple…

Monday Morning
"Your task is not to seek love, but merely to seek and find all the barriers within yourself that you have built against it."
- Jalal ad-Din Rumi

I want to text that to him. But I'm debating. I need to learn to live boldly. No wavering allowed. I want to skydive and have the wind pick me up just in time. Press send.

Thursday
It's September. I called Him to extend an offer of dinner. The little brother and I have started a catering company to raise money for his college tuition. I thought I could bring Him a plate to get his co-workers to order food from us. Networking. He should support right? He declined. He likes his food fresh; it was cooked 6 hours ago. Nevermind that he's eaten at iHop or any restaurant for that matter. He doesn't trust where it came from. I was offended. I kissed him when he was sick and he doesn't trust the food that I offered for free. He could have made me sick and I'm still offering my heart out in the form of a soul food dinner platter. I jokingly took the jab he had opened himself up for and "we" got wounded real quick. He simply pointed out, I wasn't sick.

"How would you know, you haven't checked to see how I'm doing."
"Why would you say that? You just made me sad."
His whole tone changed. Then I asked him to come see me tonight. "Like no, really just for 10 minutes."

"I'll see what I can do."

That's his way of telling me no, without saying no. I'm playing myself and somehow find myself apologizing when I didn't need to. He doesn't care. He doesn't care. He doesn't care. He ended the conversation with "we'll talk." Hmph. I'm exasperated. Hung. Spent. Can't make up my own damn mind. Waiting. Pacing. Dying. Emotional overload. I care too much, for someone who can care less. Where do I end?

3 hours later

I think I found the ending. My ending. I finally found my tears. All those emotions that are wound up in me, I can finally finally cry it out, let go of the sea of frustration. All it took was Sheldon asking me, "yo, do you believe in reciprocity?" I just need to hear a man say it rather than Lauryn. I was finished and the sea water flowed. It's not past tense...yet. But I just have to accept that it's not the right time. I could very well be the right one. Yes, that one. But timing is everything. I'm not even complete. Things I need to work on. Getting closer with God, is a good one to begin with. Move baby move. I have to let things be natural and there are just too many components I'm not happy with. Let me work on those. Goodbye my dear. There may be a later, but there are no promises.

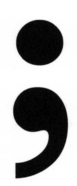

One Week Later (Friday)

This should be the beginning of a new chapter. Actually it may be more of an inserted blank page with a semi-colon boldly splashed in the center of the page. I'm trying this thing called moving on. Though, admittedly, it's been a half-assed adventure at the expense of my tear ducts and my poor poor sternum, that's been left in a state of distressed shock. It's sore from the pounding of my anxiety ridden heart. Physically sore. My sternum hates me. It's telling me to man the fuck up and find some emotional super glue to put it back together again so it can protect my heart. Stop the madness. It's a very slow death, much like Death of a Salesman, in the literal sense, where tragic human flaw renegades through the copiously depressed Willy Loman. And we're left with a protagonist who we want to love but can't, because he is a man of stupid decisions.

Won't let go of the past so he can't see his future.

I found my salesman in the tragically beautiful Him. Who's gonna save his soul now? Maybe a jumpoff or one of his female recruits or maybe even a sweet little Japanese woman who lives near Okinawa. I wonder if Afghani women are down for the Black man? And that is all I can do. Wonder.

Wonder about the ending. Concoct my sweet little detrimental fantasies that make me feel just okay. Because I can do better. I let my past go, just so I could see my future. And I believe it will be bright. That's why they call me Solì B.elieves.

6 hour drunken ellipses to beating a dead horse. I'm turning into the ex sending late night texts, cause I don't know how to let go. Damn Drake. The text that I just hit send on:

Possibly you could have been sincere. And there's just something beyond me. Or maybe you just don't want to play the bad guy so you keep me hanging. Either way, I hope you find whatever it is that you're looking for in life. I don't want you to end up lonely like the rest that I've left behind . I was in like with your potential. And there's a lot there. Use it.

(Another Four Days Pass)

I'm falling for the melodrama. I may run out of punctuation before we ever get to "." the end. Expensing all my hyphenations for the repeat of the same conversation. Inklings of moving on, by busying myself with me and somehow I get pulled back in with the warm touch over my lower back, a sly grin and Daytime Emmy-worthy (cause this is strictly for the soap operas) soliloquy that was a half reply to my punctuated text. All started by a call of "hey, I'm in your neighborhood." Hopeless, like a penny with a hole in it, again, as I shuffle my ass over to Applebee's to meet him. Hopeless, this duo of constipated love, as he tells me a tirade of what kind of man he wants to be, the kind of man he's been to his past loves and the kind of man he really he is, all of which he's only willing to give to me (at this moment) in words not in actions. Because timing is a bitch that leaves me in a pendulum of patience and angst, not taking it personal and just saying fuck you! He sucks and I emphatically tell him that. Right before going in for more...kisses that is. I wish I could sing like Amy Winehouse, then at least this crackhead status that he's depleted me to wouldn't be such a worthless state. I could croon sweet blues over Remi Salaam's drums and maybe this sad story wouldn't sound so damn pathetic. It could then be as enchanting as I've placed it in my mind, because horns make everything sound so sweet.

(That Saturday, *4 am*)

Everybody is mad at me. And I'm still left unsatisfied with the liquor warming my cool veins, entering into my brain, leaving me yearning for the touch of.... I resolve to send no more drunken texts. No more closing statements or contrite arguments in my defense. I shall meander down the road while listening to all those who care. You know, the people who really care that I will dismiss as soon as some milk chocolate, half decent, intelligent dick crosses my path of emotionally worn (but I just wanna loooove you) pussy. Yeah those folks, they call them friends, as they sit on the sideline of this asinine love/lust tale and tell me that I'm a fool. Shake their heads in shame, while telling me they still love me. Telling me to grow up, suck it up and move on. No, "delete that nigga." "Don't put your eggs all in one basket, Solì." "Make him want you." Brightening my biggest failure: my inability to play the game. I wear my emotions on my sleeve and act on my own heart. I emote feeling H-A-R-D. And this holding back, metering with patience is forever killing my soul.

(Three Odd Weeks Later)

I'm losing my sense of timing in hope that I can ease this all into a perfect little box that will be just in time for Christmas. I'm re-exhausting myself all over again. Because he called and left a silly little message singing highly off key to Maxwell's "Fistful of Tears." A mockery of a song that so perfectly expresses how I feel. I didn't answer or respond. He calls the next day. I didn't answer but I did respond, against my word of waiting for a third phone call. Clearly, I can never resist the set up. The set up that leaves me sleeping the day away just dreaming of what it could be, what I want it to be, what I need it to be. Daydreaming of a melody that sounds similar to the Cotton theme, the touch...oh yeah, the feel. I still ain't getting it. I responded the day after. He's in Miami. By himself. He wanted to know if I got his message. "Is that Maxwell's next single?" Oh, he just had to sing it. So he called. Did I get the message? "What's going on Solì B.? Is everything ok? Is everything ok Solì B? What's going on?"

The cold melts. Because I had to tell him of the incident in the cab the night before which was the reason I melted down to call him in the first place. That incident left me feeling cold and wildly alone. I have no one to stand up for me. That interesting precipice of throwing out there "I have a boyfriend" and all of sudden there's a new world of respect, and lines that aren't crossed. Yeah, that I don't have. And it all came crashing down on the Westside Highway and 44th street. So I had to tell him. And we talk about life as if everything is okay, and we're really just chum chum. And for a moment I'm left elated, that twinkle in the eye, that I've spent the past few days trying to preserve by sleeping and dreaming, occasionally roaming the city to walk and daydream.

Can you still see my twinkle? I'm worried it might run away. Run away with the days he again lets pass without a thought or a care towards me. It's been a little over three weeks, I think, since I last saw him. That languid night at Applebee's. Left with a voicemail of off key singing and a waning twinkle. I'm still waiting for him to light my fire. Don't let me burn out before then.

The End of October

He called me today. Another three weeks gone by. I took my time responding. The giddy and sprung teenybopper in me is dying a slow death with the latent effort. "Hey Mamacita, what's been going on?" I mumbled and tumbled some non-answer and he quickly flipped the script on what he perceived as my non-appreciation of his "effort." The effort that I can barely see. The effort that lands me a call in three weeks spurts with the expectancy that I should jump up and down and do backflips. Yeah, not so much. I'm "poking" him, he claims. I wonder if he got that phrase from his newly acquired Facebook page? Poking you? Makes him not want to call me because I make him feel bad about himself. No, that's you making yourself feel bad because you know you're wrong. I do nothing, other than state the obvious. He offers to help me with my Arabic. Let's see if he remembers. Child games. No new plans. I'm still sleeping in the cold. Touché, my dear, touché.

Halloween

I saw him. Like a thief in the night, literally, he walked past me, as Tia and I walked past Sugarcane. I didn't recognize him. He was crisply tanned black and I had muddled him so far into the back of my mind after that last phone call that I wasn't at all expecting to see him. I looked right passed him. Quite like he's looked right pass me over the past three months. It wasn't intentional. Just ironic. I gave him a half hug, purposefully poked him, before he yoked me up. He talks differently to me when we're in person.

That readiness to sternly shut me down isn't there when we're face to face. Somehow I feel like just maybe he does care. Pandora's box of my hopeless hope opens, again. Because I call him the following day to take him up on his offer on Arabic. Seriously, for me, I'm going to get focused. Real focused. So rather than bother him about his lack of whatever it may be that day, lets talk Arabic my dear. I can do it without him, and I'm going to do it either way, but I was hoping. Hoping that this could be a reason for real friendship. It's this hope that leads me to disappointment.

THE END-ing

cue Erykah Badu's Green Eyes
My eyes are green with tears that my heart wants to pour out. Pour out in hopes of ridding myself of all emotions and hope that I had for this one.

I'm insecure, but I can't help it.
My mind says move on.
My heart left behind...

70

I called him to hang. That thing I do so easily with my homeboys, the real ones. Talk, chop it up, see where life is leading you. Hang. But he has a date. Not a "date" per se, but ya know I would be the third wheel if I came along. Sledgehammer to my sternum, my heart swells as he clicks goodbye. He's moved on and I'm left behind.

I'm so confused you tried to trick me...

The beat drops and I really just don't understand. How someone can just walk away/run away/ignore/ deny/ suppress a feeling that's just so strong. Am I crazy? Did I feel that all on my own? Were his words just lies and a way of pacifying? What is this monster it's become? Why is my heart failing me? Where is my endurance, my strength, my will...my love?

Never thought I would but I got dissed.
Makes me feel so sad and hurt inside.
Feel embarrassed so I want to hide.

I remember the instant that I fell. I wanted to be cloaked in that feeling of mutual openness. I wanted it to be sincerely pure and true and I meant every word I ever said to him. I thought if I kissed him deep enough he would understand how true my feelings are...how harmless it is to embrace it. How easy and breezy it could all be. I fell not for the person that he presented to me, but that person I saw in the candor of his smile, the hint of creativity and humor in the twinkle of his eye. The world of potential that he was bridling underneath his Marine Corp exterior. I saw a hint of his heart, the caring, the giving, the warmth and I wanted to give that all back to him.

Silly me I thought you're love was true
Change my name to silly [Soli B.]

All I wanted to do was care and he care about me in return. Not this torrid discussion of relationships and commitment, as those take time. I wanted him to be open and honest about his emotions. Lets just build baby. I just want someone to hold me. Hot cocoa nights with laughs and kisses.

But he wants none of it. And I can't convince.
I thought if all I let out was good and sincere with a pure heart, that I would get some reciprocity. I got none of it but a tear stained pillow and a heart that's so heavy that it's plunging into my right lung. inhale. exhale. It causes me to cry every time I take a breath. I failed.
Now what do I learn from this? How do I improve myself ?
Funny, I found a postcard sent to my Great- Grandmother yesteryear.

Dated 1949, Camp Lejeune.
From her nephew Pvt. Frank A. Robinson, US Marine Corps.
It listed the Marine Corp leadership traits. First one:

72

Know yourself and seek self-improvement.

I just don't know myself anymore.
Before I heal it's going to be a while,
I know it's going to be a while chile'
la di la di di daaaa...

21 Days

I did it again. It feels like, God put out an order this year to stone my heart or maybe it's the laws of the universe reaping sweet revenge for what I don't know. It just took twenty one days for my sternum to feel like it was being pummeled. Drop kick to the chest, caught completely off guard. No clue. No indication. Stunned.

Ashton, a Texas bred, crooked front teeth, outdated style, college football player who cooked me dinner on the third night, slept with me on the fifth night and left sweet kisses on my forehead. I thought he was cool, amidst the questionable physicality and the ability to snore like an impending tornado in the Great Plains. I liked him, enough. Well, really I liked the sex and the convenience, and the sex...alot. I got caught, even though again, I knew better. I met all his friends and coworkers. We talked a lot. He opened up about his life. I kept it tepid. And I thought it was good. Twenty one days.

Then boom. I cooked him steak. Wrote his final term paper for him. Ho shit, for someone who I enjoyed more for the sex than his actual personality. I was trying to sit on the fence about it. Ha, I guess I played Humpty Dumpty. Fell off the damn fence and no one came to scoop me up. No good Samaritan to help me along the way. I'm left crumbled on the desert floor. Don't make no sense.

I can't begin to explain how it feels to be so blindsidedly disrespected out the blue with no rhyme or reason. As you play over and over again the actions leading up to the incident. It wasn't even a matter of my heart. He went straight for my soul and threw a lit match on it without even looking back. I can't fathom the cause, the reason, the affect. I can't fathom how someone can be so careless when 36 hours before they cared so much. It makes no sense. I settled for less and thought in his corniness I would find reprieve from the usual asshole cadence. I knew it wasn't going to work out. But I thought at the very least when he caught the itching for some new pussy he would be nice enough to put me down more gently with at least a hint of respect. Why go so out of your way to deal with me, even after you got the draws. Why the sweet kisses on my forehead, talks of the future, bringing me into your social circle of close friends? Why the cooked dinner, the offer to do my laundry, asking when you can come to my place? Wait, why do I have keys to your place? Passwords to all your email accounts? I wouldn't even do those things unless it was someone I trusted and wanted to be around, someone who I wholeheartedly wanted to incorporate into my life.

Tuesday, that would be five days ago, I hit Ashton about the papers, kept it cool; I knew he was on lock down for his finals. Asked him about Christmas Eve since I had invited him to Brooklyn for that evening. He gave me the set up of 'he might not be able to make it but he'll keep me updated'. Then from someone who usually hits me up everyday, leaves voice messages detailing a play by play of his day and would be offended if I skipped a day in talking to him, he doesn't hit me up. Christmas Eve rolls around and nothing. Struck me as odd, but maybe he's just really, really, really busy. Or maybe he's just really, really, really high. Or maybe I'm just really, really, really too damn forgiving, gullible, impatient and not ready. So I call. He answers. Sweetly feeds me a crop of bull about a not working phone (because he dropped it) but he was able to contact his homeboys for drinks and then end up in Philly on Christmas. Oh he knows he was suppose to keep me updated but he has to go back, they about to eat, he had to step out to talk to me, but he'll be back tonight, he'll call me later. I didn't get it. It made no sense. I hear nothing again for the rest of Christmas, no contact on the day after. There's something not right. I know its not me. I smell bullshit.

The clock struck midnight, and why I felt the need to check his Facebook profile, I do not know. But I did and he had posted a picture of a lightskin, wavy chick lying in his lap, captioned "hmmm, to be goofy or not to be goofy," then made it his profile picture. Damn social media and all of its corniness. Damn his blatant, boastful disrespect that caught silly me out of the blue. I called him twice. Twice, I was sent to voicemail. I've been played. Again, my dear.

I don't know whether to me mad, upset or whether I just feel like the complete fool. Wait, were there feelings attached or do I just feel disrespected? Part of me wants to laugh, like laughing at a funeral. I got got and it makes no sense.

I feel like the scourged rags my father use to keep to clean the deep thick car grease off his hands. I fucked a cornball. I let a cornball blow my back out and hurt my feelings with a swift blow of disrespect. I was mad, livid, pissed, flashes of red with contempt and the fact that this fool lucked out. Yep, he lucked out with my belief in karmic return and just allowing him to move on. Damnit, damnit, damnit! I could have gotten him so good. Cut his balls off and played handball with them. Slammed them against the wall and watch them sliver down the backboard. Gobbity gop. I'm smiling.

Instead I was tossed with no care. No thought. No clue. Twenty-one days I lived in a cool bliss, and yesterday I was dropped from my cloud. Just didn't realize it had gotten that high. I just want to say good bye to 2009.

Over That

I sat right behind him. I knew he would be there. I had to go, just so I could kick him in the balls with a curt smile and a nonchalant, "Hey Ashton," while he's sitting next to what I'm assuming is his girlfriend's family. The same girl from his Facebook profile pic that he put up the day after Christmas. The day after he lied to me. The same girl who he tagged in the picture to let the whole social media world know who she was. The same girl whose profile I clicked on and realized she was in my homeboy's theatre company. Gotcha. Because even though I'm trying to be on my grown woman swag, and literal revenge is now out of the question, I have to grab you by the balls one last time. I'm a fiend for reactions. I couldn't let his blatant and flagrant disrespect go. Oh no, that is not allowed.

I was in a particularly good mood that day. Stars were aligning in a magnificent way for my career and I was riding high on some great news. Plus, it's always delightful to be able to so quickly get over someone when you realize how beneath you they really are. God always finds a good way to kick me in the ass when I start to settle for less than. That profile pic was a good way to kick me. Kick me hard. There was no passion or great sweeping emotion. There was just the coolness of convenience and some good sex on a regular. But I was still sore over the Marine, so he got to me too. A damn waste.

So when that homeboy's theatre company put on a show, I was there to support. Duality in tack. I got there late, ending up in a seat right behind him. Saw the oversized cubic zirconia stuck in his cartilage (that should have been a big sign to just say NO from the door), as soon as I walked in. Show was great. It's a small auditorium. There's some other folks I know. I say hi to them first right in his view, so he can have a second to compose himself, then I politely turn around, knock him upside his shoulder with a quick slap. I didn't mean for it to be so hard, but it popped right off his corduroy blazer (circa NeYo 2004, it's 2010 dear) and his face dropped. Just for a quick second then he stepped back, pulled it together and managed out a "oh hi, how you doing?" "Great!" Kept it moving to my other associates and he darted out of there, head down, hands in pocket.

It's all good boo. I won't be coming for you anymore. You're old news. A snooze. An L I just had to take to close out 2009. I just had to instill the fear with my curt smile. Job done. You're done. Over that.

I wish it was the same over that for others.

A Woo Woo Woo

Susan Miller just had to be right. Even if I try to sugarcoat my belief in the stars by saying I take astrology with a grain of salt, Ms. Miller always comes a-roaring with a prophetic kick in the ass. She said in the Aries monthly horoscope for December, that I would (because I'm the only Aries in the world) have a relationship that would completely blindside me, and I would get dropped like hot grease with no rhyme or reason. I was destined to not find out until after April 10th. Sure enough without a doubt, Ms. Miller proved correct. There's no explanation for this. To think every dude I've ever been with has given a half ass apology in some curt fashion. My first with a red microwave. James in a languid email response to my weeping willow saying that he needs "to get [his] shit together, sorry." Conrad after my dash to be the heartbreaker first, and Kenna when I was only half listening cause time just wouldn't let us be, apologized for not being able to give me what I deserve. Then there's Ashton. A good fuck, close to great fuck, who pulled a wammy in 21 days that caused me to be quite over that. His timing was impeccable.

A transcript of out G-Chat conversation:

1:51 PM Chat with Ashton:
Ashton: What up punk...is the first thing you do when u see me again, is slap me again?

me: Are you being serious?

86

Ashton: No, I feel like u could have done worse...but I really couldn't think of anything to say more than hello as an opener

me: I'm dying of laughter right now...this makes no damn sense
Why are you hitting me up?

Ashton: I was going to somehow transition into a long overdue apology for the way things left off, and to see how u were

me: ahhhhh...an apology 4 months later, this is flat out hilarious

Funny enough...since I believe in horoscopes...this was in my monthly horoscope.

Was wondering how it was going to come about

Why you apologizing now?

Ashton: Better late than never...no real reason...just felt like I should

1:57 PM

me: But why....what are you really sorry about?

Ashton: It was inappropriate the way things just left off at a dead end...I at least owed u an explanation

Well not an explanation but some sort of communication other than cutting u off

me: And what would that communication have been?

Ashton: It's easier typed than said and done, considering how things were progressing between us...in that we would have to be platonic friends because my ex, who I had been in touch with over the last year, were getting back together

me: You got a lot of growing up to do because seriously I could have had you by the balls. you just lucked out with timing and me knowing that I got way better things to focus my energy on.
Quite frankly I knew what it was...from the gate, and I do remember calling you out on your bs, but you denied it and wanted to do all that fanciful talking...etc.

Basically without going into a whole diatribe, really that whole situation was just a matter of convenience for both of us and I knew it was going to end when whoever found the next best thing first

Ashton: If that is the way you see it then so be it

me: But for you to be in contact with someone who you wanted to get back with...just for future reference...don't EVER wrap a chick up that much in your life. If I had no shame I could have done a lot of embarrassing. I'm not mad at the whole situation...I was just in awe of the blatant disrespect...like who involves someone that much in their daily life and not take care to be respectful so it doesn't come back and bite them in they ass.
That is what it is for me.

Ashton: But I have no reason to lie, embellish 4 months later...you're right you did ask me about it...and I gave the answer I felt...if I didn't enjoy the time I wouldn't have spent that much with you.

I understand that perfectly...

me: You did lie

2:15 PM

Ashton: Which is why I said I owed you an apology

me: That whole situation on your end was a lie

It's cool

Ashton: No I didn't

I said I was looking for something more serious and was...though I was in contact with my ex yes...but it had been a year...I didn't know where it was going I very much appreciate the way you handled stuff and I'm not knocking you for that look...

I wanted to apologize...you don't have to accept it...I understand the circumstances...I'm just saying is all

me: I get it ... got it

4 months ago when it happened

you carry no weight to me....I appreciate the apology.... trust me, there will be no burning of balls I knew what it was as soon as I saw it I just think you were not at all mature in that situation and I was damn fool for going with it, when I knew better. But hey it is what it is.

So lets call it even....this never happened....and life goes on....I guess you can feel better about yourself now....I hope life works out for you

Hey it is the year of karmic return ;)

Oh, and I hope you got a really good grade on that paper

Ashton: Lol thanks for the karma wish...and the paper

was a B...not bad...I coulda got an A ;)

me: lolol ok

Ashton: glad to know I'm amusing and you don't hate me ;)

me: lol.....hate is reserved only for people you can touch a special place in my heart...that's a waste of energy
you sure are presumptuous

4:43 PM
Ashton: wow ok

aight imma get back to work

The following day...
Chat with Ashton
3:08 PM (19 minutes ago)

3:08 PM
Ashton: So, am I still just a ghost of the past to you?

me: what's ur intentions?

Ashton: just saying hello is all draw the talons back

me: draw the claws back? loll

Ashton: just sayin sheesh

me: I just don't understand why you care....

I'm tryin to understand your logic

Ashton: doesn't have a life threatening stance...just a stance...I just generally get along with everyone

me: true...I generally get along with everyone as well, but I'm generally not a straight bitch to people either, so ya know :)

Ashton: yeah I know...well guess the apology card was played so....aight enjoy your day

PMS in
September

I'm trying to drown my depression in the bottom of this bottle of wine. It's not working just yet. My tear ducts are stopped up. Can't cry but I have a knot in my chest and feel soulless. PMSing at its finest. I only PMS like this during the month of September. It's the month of life decisions. The 6-month marker of my birthday. That point where I always stop and think how far I have come in all the promises that I made to myself. Did I ever imagine I would be living life like this? Gosh, I think I'm beginning to hate September.

At 25, life was not supposed to be like this. I shouldn't be living in Bushwick surrounded by Mexicans, who don't speak a lick of English. My heart longing to go back to Bedstuy and instead settling for cheap rent and my growing obsession with tacos. At 25, I shouldn't be broke and so damn lonely. I shouldn't be in my room at 4pm drinking a bottle of cheap wine and typing away my heart. Shit, I don't really know what I'm lamenting over. I thought I was over this. Thought I had picked up the pieces of my busted ego, heart, id, superego and pride last September when it all went smattering down with two screaming phone calls. Thought I realized, I couldn't catch a break cause my time just hadn't come...yet. Thought I was good. I'm not good. I'm better, but not good. Slightly bitter, jaded, faded and hurt.

Last September, a year to the date, landing the 7th of the month. I clearly remember the Saturday, walking down

Fulton St. past Brooklyn Academy of Music, coming around from Atlantic Center. Up past Habana Outpost , while I was in my PMSing mood of calculating my life, trying to figure out what pieces needed to be sanded down, rounded out and put some place else to get my life together as soon as possible. That January, I had put all my career eggs in one basket, behind an Atlanta rapper named Ty Billz. Helped his manager, Josh, drag him out of the trap(s); literally, the crack houses and dope corners of Pink City, Zone 3, Atlanta. Spent late nights, convincing Josh to have more of a heart and stick with a belligerent grown ass man, who had talent but didn't believe in its ability to take him that far. Other days were spent stalking bloggers and cashing in on all my IOUs collected over five years of hustling in the music industry. Just a month before September, after 6 months of convincing them that they needed a visual aid to Ty's mixtape, I spent another 3 hours convincing Josh to not cancel the video shoot for Ty's "Trap on Fire." Josh was doing his usual bitching over money and all of his dedication, ending with me canceling my plane ticket to Atlanta. My rent was due and these two fools were still bickering with no finale in sight. A week after the fact the video is done and by September it was quickly becoming a viral success. As I watched all of our collaborative work turn into a reverently growing buzz, I just knew all my eggs were going to hatch.

Pity the fool that was I, waiting on the return of my good karma. Taking the gamble of all my eggs in one basket, being harvested by a man with a severe case of bitchassness. This wasn't the one click game of Farmville. This was my life and integrity. I saw it coming and it hit me like a ton of bricks. Late August, with the buzz solidifying into meetings with record labels, the classic "boys club swindle" was to be my demise. I should of saved one of my eggs, right after that meeting with Asylum Records, the label known for its quick turnover with niche, mildly successful southern rappers. They were all eyeing me, knowing that I would be the deterrence to a quick deal. Too smart for my own good. Walked out the office, with the smoke and mirrors of dollar signs with thorns glistening in Josh and Ty's eyes. Hooked to the fast cash with a handshake and dap, past the dotted line, I was overshadowed. Me and my basket were soon to be dropped.

It's September 7th, 2009 and I'm still walking up Fulton St., coming past Habana Outpost, calculating all the work I've done for two fools. One fool, Josh, always said he rocked with me "off the strength" the strength of honesty and integrity of my word in a industry full of shady people. (False) Promises of Josh doing the same in return. I was the fool for listening. The fool for believing. Then I decided to call the fools. I couldn't just let this go. I noticed the deterring frequency in correspondence with Josh. Folks walking up to me on the street telling me things about Ty Billz that I should of heard from Josh. I was being played the fool, my basket of eggs thrown out the car window. I picked up the phone and called. Right on Fulton St. and S. Portland, I started walking in circles as I waited for Josh to answer. Call connected.

The next 8 minutes are a blur of me angrily pacing down the blocks of Ft. Greene, beseeching Josh to admit that he was dropping me. Dropping me because dollar signs were now in the air. Mase ain't lie, more money more problems, right? Josh can't find his tongue so he puts Ty on the phone, because all he could muster was a "Solì it's complicated now...we just can't, we just can't" and a bunch of other incomplete sentences. Ty gets on the phone, offering a quick blow to my chest. "Solì, what have you done for me other than introduce to me a few bloggers that I already knew." My sense of self is being splattered with egg. Splitting my ego, shattering my pride. I dropped the phone. I wanted to scream, run from Fort Greene, Brooklyn all the way to Downtown Atlanta, Jones St. and kick the door into Josh's cushy loft apartment and choke the shit out of both of them. Shake them into understanding all the work that I had put wholeheartedly behind this project, without asking for a dime. They dropped me before that dime could even be considered because they were scared that they would have to share. In that moment I watched all the work that was the center of my pride be washed away on the corner of S. Portland and Fulton Street. Watched the egg yolk run down my integrity. Chips of eggshells logged in my sense of self. This was my mighty call to say I knew what I was doing. To make all those years of hustling make sense. Cause little Solì B. actually had a focus, had something to claim as my own. My work, my doing.

A case of bitchassness turned me into a glorified intern. I was beginning to hate September. I want to blame it all on September, that even in a business relationship I couldn't get the respect. I was still being bitched out, just this time there was no sex involved. The fade to black act that men do when they don't know how to tell a girl that they're no longer interested. Mid-September, face to face I'm having this conversation with Josh in my living room, attempting to verbally shake him to realizing I'm not his bitch, I'm not a nag, was never a chick that was just good for the head. I was a part of the business venture. An integral part of the team that led Ty to a feature in the New York Times. The reason why you're being chauffeured around by Mark Ronson. The reason why Fader Magazine is doing a shoot for Ty in my living room. And all I can get out of him is that I need to "man up", yeah "man up Solì." Ty quickly cosigning while trying to reason away his illicit remark of 'what have I done for him lately' from two weeks prior, reasoning that he just wanted me to map out all that I've done so he could understand where I'm coming from. My eggs splattered all over my tile checkered living room floor. Tossed my basket out the window when I tire of the conversation, realizing that I'm just losing the war. I go to my room. I hear Josh talking with my best friend, Sheldon, telling him to talk to me cause really they just can't afford to pay me my due. My hate for September is growing.

I still thought I could salvage it by walking them into the MTV offices, and turning a short MTV News piece into a full on MTV webisode, a la the "Ty Billz Cooking Show." But that wasn't enough to even keep the lines of communication open. I should have picked my basket up and ran. Ran on the day, when some random dude I recognized but couldn't put a name to, stopped me on Nostrand Ave in December, and asked when Ty was leaving town, I shrugged it off because I didn't even know he was there. Should have saved one egg, because September had turned me into a glorified intern. No due was going to be mine. And I was taking the all around L, relegated to being a part of Josh's general population who he sends weekly email blasts about Ty Billz to. Played the same way I've been played in love relationships. I found out Ty signed to Asylum via Twitter with a blurry of "Congratulations, you've done it!" direct messages and emails from various bloggers, but none from Josh or Ty. PMSing in September turned me into the intern. Thought I would make it with them but I was left with no love, no thanks, no heart, they just snatched my basket with all my eggs away.

i

I am i.

My I has been depleted through the years. Frustration, exhaustion, lethargic apathy.
I can no longer deal and i has shuttled into its place.

Not enough pride to rock i like bell hooks, cause i still likes men. i needs solace.

I still appears on some days, when the sun is bright and there are things to do. But on most days it is i who arises to pull the comforter back over her head. i allows the anxiety to consume her, the worries of money and lost efforts drowned in a cheap bottle of Trader Joe's wine.

i's demons thrive off of technology. The faux relationships maintained through two thumbs typing away. i can maintain relationships through thumbs with no acknowledgement of emotions or true feelings. Faux friendships are developed. Laissez-faire flirting with boys who will never take the initiative. A world of people who only know i, but will never know I. My thumbs allow i to reign supreme. The sweeping smile that changes the landscape of i's face in a fleeting moment of I, for public consumption. I attempts to shine through with passion and dedication that are only meet with "Solì, you'll make" "Solì, you got it, it'll be okay" and cliché statements of pseudo care without any help. I is deflated into i.

i needs to be saved.

i needs to become I.

It's a blurry of emotion, that i/I cannot escape.

A constant struggle to reconcile my pride, ambition, humility, reality and emotions into one.

I cannot articulate my emotions. Only i can allow anything other than happy to escape and even that is only through my thumbs. My emotions can only be explained through music, though i allows my pride to become my hubris, never allowing the world to see anything other than cool Solì B. I screams from the inside, scratching, screeching to be released. A deluge of all my passion and emotions of the real me in I, that i is so afraid that no one can handle.

i is not I.

i is at lost.

I needs to be saved. Save me.

Save I.

Save...

A Long Ass Note

From: "Soli"

Subject: A Long Ass Note…

To: …

I'm finna to send this and I'm not even sure about your email or if you even read email. Lmao, someone has to read this.

Typically I send the email as soon as the shit hits the fan. Cut it off at the root, so I can get over it, learn from it , move on and try to do better. This situation was such a clusterfuck that made absolutely no sense, I didn't even know how to respond. No matter how I look at it or spin it, I just don't get how my only expectation couldn't be fulfilled. I wanted respect. And respect is not a material pursuit of you paying for fast food and cocktails.

To wit, as treacherous as a lot of women can be, your coins don't excite me. You work far too hard for your money and in the most respectful way I can put this, you don't make enough for me to even entertain the idea of laying on my back for a hamburger & banana shake or, to quell your previous concerns, to get pregnant, go through the 9months of gestation with no sex, and then push out what's guaranteed to be a big headed being out of my very tight vagina, for the prospect of nickels from you. My nigga, no…dumbest shit ever. Yes, your statement about how much you've done for me was utterly offensive.

As much as I wanted to have sympathy for your situation, in understanding that working as hard as you do and still

106

find that simple comforts aren't that simple to attain, these are not conversations that we ever had. Your wall of distrust doesn't allow for much past superficial conversations and I was okay with that because for me this was a situation of comfort and respect. A moment to exhale and just enjoy, leaving any excess baggage at the airport. I wanted to enjoy the moment so much, that when whatever was actually on your mind was so overwhelming that you had shut down from an meaningful conversation, I put my mouth on it, to relax the mood.

Yes, it's more than bothersome to me that a man, who I've opened myself to, would insinuate that I just sexually gallivant around with my various male friends. Mostly because I live in honesty. then because I genuinely do not like people, so the few I do, whether friends or ambiguous (as you put it) 'best' friend relationships, matter to me – I don't waste time. Lastly I don't have good enough medical insurance to be a hoe. You can ask about a pap smear, but ask your next fuck buddy about BV and HPV, if you really want to be informed.

I do wish you well sir. I think you're smart and have a ton of potential. Hopefully you'll find someone who will open you up to new worlds of exploration and you can benefit. Read some Paulo Coelho in the mean time.

Deuces.
Solana :)

Goodnight...

There's a million ways I hope to tell my life story.

There's a million smiles I hope to spread across my heart.

There's a bod of happiness I wish to attain, and somehow every little bit of it just misses my grip because of this one little thing. This one little thing I just can't get makes everything else taste wrong.

Makes the music sound so bad.

Leaves me fetal in my cold ass bed and a weeping willow on a Friday night.

Leaving me wanting to scream at the top of my lungs and punch holes into various things. Never that. Never that. Never that.

I want to send belligerent soliloquies to make it all disappear. But I can't. Never that. Never that. Never that.

I just want love and somehow it keeps escaping me. And without it, all my other passions just seem dismal. Every other hope seems inadequate to attain.

And I feel like a bowl of nothingness.

All other happiness just feels worthless and I feel like the big fool. The fool, the fool my dear. That is me.

The loveless fool.

Goodnight.

Good Day,

I smile, because I know one day I'll tell Him that I LOVE Him, and it will be a beautifully genuine wonderful moment, because I learned to love me first.

- Solì B.

My Valentine's Day

Jouelzy

Somewhere between perfection and imperfection. Urban dweller from the land of suburbia, briefly assimilated into a Brooklyn doll and now a child of the wind, wherever it may move me. I live my life through music and though my story is riddled with neo-soul tales, I oscillate between the hood aesthetic and well-read bourgeoisie. You can find me on any given day on the internets with my heart on my sleeves and my emotions written all over my face, hopefully inspiring young women to live freely in their skin. I am vulnerable and tough as nails. The perfect contradiction of the imperfect human.

www.jouelzy.com
Join the conversation, we welcome your feedback
@jouelzy

CPSIA information can be obtained
at www.ICGtesting.com
Printed in the USA
LVHW090914241118
598132LV00001B/316/P